Parents and Caregivers,

Stone Arch Readers are designed to provide enjoyable reading experiences, as well as opportunities to develop vocabulary, literacy skills, and comprehension. Here are a few ways to support your beginning reader:

- Talk with your child about the ideas addressed in the story.

- Discuss each illustration, mentioning the characters, where they are, and what they are doing.

- Read with expression, pointing to each word. You may want to read the whole story through and then revisit parts of the story to ensure that the meanings of words or phrases are understood.

- Talk about why the character did what he or she did and what your child would do in that situation.

- Help your child connect with characters and events in the story.

Remember, reading with your child should be fun, not forced. Each moment spent reading with your child is a priceless investment in his or her literacy life.

Gail Saunders-Smith, Ph.D.

STONE ARCH **READERS**

are published by Stone Arch Books, a Capstone Imprint
151 Good Counsel Drive, P.O. Box 669
Mankato, Minnesota 56002
www.capstonepub.com

Library of Congress Cataloging-in-Publication data
is available on the Library of Congress website.
ISBN: 978-1-4342-2052-3 (library binding)
ISBN: 978-1-4342-2794-2 (paperback)

Summary: It's pet day at school. Jake can't wait to show his class all the
tricks his dog, Buddy, can do. What will be Buddy's best trick?

Reading Consultants:
Gail Saunders-Smith, Ph.D.
Melinda Melton Crow, M.Ed.
Laurie K. Holland, Media Specialist

Art Director: Kay Fraser
Designer: Emily Harris
Production Specialist: Michelle Biedscheid

The Best Trick

A **PET CLUB** STORY

by Gwendolyn Hooks

illustrated by Mike Bryne

STONE ARCH BOOKS
a capstone imprint

Lucy, Jake, Kayla, and Andy are best friends. Lucy has a rat named Ajax. Jake has a dog named Buddy.

Kayla has a cat named Daisy.
Andy has a fish named Nibbles.
Together, they are the Pet Club!

Today is pet day at school.
Everyone is excited.

The Pet Club is extra excited.

Andy brings his fish. Lucy brings
her rat. Kayla brings her cat.
Jake brings his dog.

Jake can't wait for show-and-tell.
Buddy has lots of tricks.

First the class has to do math
and spelling.

Finally Mr. Carter says, "It's time for show-and-tell!"

Andy goes first.

"This is Nibbles. She swims and blows bubbles," Andy says.

"Your tricks are better," Jake says to Buddy.

Kayla goes next.

"This is Daisy. She can climb trees," Kayla says.

"Your tricks are better," Jake says to Buddy.

Lucy goes next.

"This is Ajax. He can move his whiskers," Lucy says.

"Your tricks are better," Jake says
to Buddy.

At last, it's Jake's turn. Jake goes
to the front of the room. He tosses
a ball.

"Get the ball, Buddy," Jake says.

Buddy just sits and wags his tail.

"Lie down," Jake says.

Buddy just sits and wags his tail.

"Roll over," Jake says.

Buddy just sits and wags his tail.
Jake's time is up.

Jake feels sad. Buddy did not do
his tricks.

Mr. Carter says, "It's time for lunch."

Buddy runs across the room.

He does not get the ball. He does
not roll over.

Buddy gets Jake's backpack.

"What do you have?" Jake asks.
Buddy has Jake's lunch.

Everyone cheers for Buddy.

Buddy knows the best trick of all!

STORY WORDS

school	tricks	climb
excited	swims	whiskers
show-and-tell	bubbles	backpack

Total Word Count: 275

Join the Pet Club today!

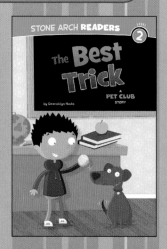